Look for these other books in the Commander Kellie and the Superkids™ Adventure Series:

D1531576

Commander Kellie and the Superkids™

#1

The Mysterious Presence

Christopher P.N. Maselli

KENNETH
COPELAND
PUBLICATIONS

The Mysterious Presence

ISBN-10 1-57562-215-7   30-0901
ISBN-13 978-1-57562-215-6

19 18 17 16 15 14   13 12 11 10 9 8

© 1999 Kenneth Copeland Ministries

Kenneth Copeland Publications
Fort Worth, TX 76192-0001

Larry Warren/artist

Dedication

For Superkids
everywhere...

Contents

Hello Superkid!

My name is Alex Taylor and something extraordinary just happened to me.

I discovered a secret room in Superkid Academy—and you won't believe what I found inside of it.

First, you should understand that Superkid Academy is where I live. I came here a few years ago and joined the Blue Squad for my training. Life has been an adventure ever since.

There are four other Superkids in the Blue Squad with me: Paul, Missy, Rapper and Valerie. Of course, there's also our robot, Techno. Our commander is Commander Kellie—and she's the best at the Academy. God always takes the seven of us on the wildest adventures you can imagine. As we put our faith in Him and His Word, He never lets us down!

This particular adventure started not long ago, when, as I said, I discovered this mysterious, hidden room in the Academy. Since Superkid Academy is located in a building that used to belong to NME (an outspoken foe of ours) there was no telling what we'd find behind its walls. So we just put our faith in God and trusted that He would give us the answer. What we encountered was the last thing I expected...

Had I not discovered the power of praise and the presence of the Lord...well...I don't even want to think about it.

This is my story...

Alex

The Mysterious Presence

Something Mysterious

Fa-TOOM!

Dust filled the small hallway as a hole near the floor about the size of a trash can lid crumbled away from the wall. A nearby ventilation grate spit out dust, too, further filling the hallway with a smoky atmosphere.

"Detonation complete," Paul announced, pulling down his safety goggles, letting them dangle from his neck. Commander Kellie and the four Superkids behind her followed his example.

"Well done, Paul." The commander reached forward and squeezed his arm. Behind her, Missy coughed and muttered something about the dust. Rapper was smiling, satisfied with the explosion. Valerie brushed sandy, white granules from her shoulder-length, brown hair. Finally, in the back, Alex scratched his curly hair and listened to Techno finish the report.

"Detonation of coordinates 15-49 successful," the robot offered, whirring. His smooth, yet boxy, snow-white body rolled forward to gain further diagnostics.

"What's back there?" Alex wondered, pointing to the darkness behind the new hole.

"Just oxygen and the dust we created with the explosion," Techno reported. "It should be safe to enter."

"Now, Superkids," Commander Kellie addressed them firmly, "this looks rather routine. But I don't have to remind you about the dangers a mission like this could entail. Because our headquarters is located in an old NME building, there's no telling what we're going to find in a secret room like this. So let's be cautious. Remember 1 Peter 5:8-9—'Be self-controlled and alert. Your enemy the devil prowls around like a roaring lion looking for someone to devour. Resist him, standing firm in faith.'"

Alex gulped. He loved the adventure of being on Superkid Academy's most experienced ministry team, the Blue Squad...but the risks he was asked to take were sometimes a little faith-stretching (to say the least). This mission was no exception.

The day before, during a routine computer system checkup, Alex noticed an unmarked area on a holographic map of Superkid Academy. When he showed it to Commander Kellie, she made it top priority to find out what was in the mysterious, unexplored area. Now, here they were, next to the hidden room and they had securely blasted a hole into it. Somehow, Alex now wished he hadn't found the room in the first place. But he couldn't let it go unnoticed—for one very obvious reason: NME.

The Notoriously Malicious Enterprises (NME) organization existed for one purpose: to instill fear in children with the hope of one day controlling them. This objective, of course, made NME an instant adversary of Superkid

Academy. The Superkids were devoted to proclaiming the Truth, sharing God's Word and instilling faith (the opposite of fear) into kids everywhere.

Every day, it seemed, NME was up to something new and more evil. The Superkids' duties included interrupting NME television broadcasts and generally fouling up their evil plans whenever possible—anything to prevent the darkness from spreading. Meanwhile, their ultimate goal was to share the power of God's Word with the world. Needless to say, with NME on the loose, such a task was challenging sometimes...and at other times, it was just plain dangerous.

Danger was the reason that, eight months earlier, Superkid Academy was forced to move its headquarters. NME was close to discovering the hidden base, but a plan of Commander Kellie's left them wandering in circles.

The commander suggested transferring their hideout to the last possible place NME would look for them—and the very next day, the Academy began its move to an old NME headquarters building. It was a brilliant plan and NME was still in the dark...but Alex had found something peculiar. Something that made the Superkids wonder if NME still had some ties to their old building. Alex had found this unmapped room in the center of the building. So, without a doubt, finding out what was inside immediately became a top-priority mission for Superkid Academy's Blue Squad.

Since it was top priority, everything else was put on hold. This, of course, included Alex's birthday—his eleventh birthday. *Oh, well,* Alex thought, *sometimes celebrating has to wait. Meanwhile, back to work!*

The part Alex liked best about his training was working with his companions. He knew they probably saw him as a techno-geek sometimes since he hung around the Superkids' robot, Techno, and his computer so much. But that didn't matter. As a team, each one of them was responsible for being the best they could be in their assigned area. And they were all *great* friends.

Alex looked at the Blue Squad and felt a surge of satisfaction. Heading the group was Commander Kellie. With her straight, brown hair bound in a ponytail, she stood confidently in her royal blue and gold expedition uniform. A utility belt sporting mostly empty pockets (where clay explosives had earlier found their home) was tightened around her waist. Alex reserved a special place in his heart for Commander Kellie—an adult with the adventurous drive of a kid. A leader of leaders, she had helped each of the Superkids look to God to find truth. He felt he'd always be indebted to her.

Paul and Missy were the two older Superkids. Both teens stood tall and had blond hair, though Missy's was noticeably fancier. Paul wore a utility belt like Commander Kellie's, but Missy wore a simple, royal-blue, leather belt around her uniform like the other Superkids. Paul was the handsome, natural leader of the group—born with street smarts and ready for action. When Commander Kellie wasn't around, everyone could count on Paul to call the shots wisely. Beautiful

Missy, on another scale, was from uptown. Everything about her was high-class—from her manicured fingernails to her bright red lipstick. She had a strong spirit and she was never at a loss for words.

Rapper was a couple inches shorter than Paul, with cropped, brown hair and a constant smile. He was one of the Academy's best pilots, and, of course, he loved to rap. Valerie, a dark brunette, was about Rapper's height and had a simple, natural beauty. At times, when she stood with her hands on her hips, one could argue that she looked remarkably like a miniature Commander Kellie. Another great pilot, Valerie was sure to realize her dream of being a Superkid commander herself one day. Rapper and Valerie were not yet teenagers, but their maturity level reached far beyond their young years.

Among such great "heroes" of the Academy, Alex felt a little tongue-tied sometimes. With perfect, dark skin and a million-dollar smile, Alex was the youngest and, by far, the shortest in the group...but he was growing. He never abandoned his hope that one day he would be a hero, too.

Commander Kellie pulled out her flashlight—a long, black cylinder with soft, touch-pad buttons that gave the user the option of several brightness levels. Alex wasn't looking forward to entering the dingy, unknown place. Sure, there might be nothing at all beyond the thick, foreboding wall, but the NME organization used to own the building. And Alex wanted nothing to do with them. He'd seen for himself how they pulled innocent kids into the organization with flashy television programming... and then took away their free will...so that all that was left were lost and confused kids doing whatever NME said. If they didn't do what NME said—well, that wasn't a pleasant thought.

"Here we go!" Missy flashed a toothy and unsure smile.

"So," Commander Kellie said, holding out the flashlight, "who wants to go first?"

The room fell so quiet Alex could hear the buzzing of the round lights set in the gray ceiling above. Commander Kellie looked at Paul. Paul looked at Missy. Missy looked at Rapper. Rapper looked at Valerie. Valerie looked at Alex. Alex looked at Techno.

"I can't fit in there!" the robot whirred, his voice echoing in the hall. "Well, not unless you take my head off."

"Why don't *I* go first," the commander said, smiling. "But before I enter, let's put what we learned about praise into practice. Let's bring the presence of God on the scene."

A week earlier, during the Superkids' morning study time, their commander had begun teaching them about the power in praising and worshiping God. Alex found that praising God was nothing to be ashamed about. The Superkid Manual said in Psalm 9:1, "I will praise you, Lord, with all my heart. I will tell all the miracles you have done."

Alex was ready to praise God with his whole heart. He was ready to let God take control of the situation.

The Superkids joined together, singing a worship song Paul had written.

Early in the morning
I'll lift up songs of praise
Songs of thanks and honor
Songs of love ablaze

And late, late in the evening
I'll worship Your Holy Name
For You give me the victory
You're forever the same

Without shame, I'll worship You, my Lord
Lifting up Your Name, I'll shout Your praises
I will proclaim Your Word of victory
And I will tell of all You've done for me

Then after a brief moment of whispered, individual worship to God, Commander Kellie broke the silence and addressed the group. "I want each of you to remember that you are *Superkids*. And remember the Superkid motto: 'All things are possible with God and we can do all things through Christ which gives us strength.'" The Superkids nodded in unison, remembering the motto based on Luke 1:37 and Philippians 4:13.

Commander Kellie flashed the beam of her flash-light into the dark hole. Settling dust danced in the beam, making it look like a piercing sword of light. The commander paused a moment and tapped on her Warren Technologies Communication Watch, or "ComWatch." Paul tapped on his own watch and the display popped up with an electronic picture of Commander Kellie's face. Paul's face was on the commander's watch.

"All right." The commander brushed back a strand of her long, dark hair from her eyes. "Let's keep in touch through our ComWatches. I'll lock in with Paul's. It'll be dark, so you won't be able to see me for long, but I'll be able to see you." She pulled a pair of special infrared glasses out of her utility belt and placed them over her eyes. The small, black frames and cloudy glass made her look more like she was ready to go onto the beach rather than into a dark room. "Since I'll be able to see easier in the dark with my I-Glasses, let me give this place a look over and then you can follow."

Paul acknowledged his agreement by twisting a knob on his ComWatch, fine-tuning the link to his commander's watch. On the screen, her face became sharper, a muted beep sounded and the 14-year-old nodded his head. The commander tapped the bridge of her I-Glasses, turning them on.

"Oh, boy," Missy said with another unsure, but bright, white smile.

"Don't be afraid," Valerie whispered. Commander Kellie winked assuredly at Valerie and Alex's stomach turned as she scrunched down and entered the hole.

"Can you see me?"

"No, Commander," Paul responded to the ComWatch. The video display was black.

"Just as I thought, it's too dark. Well, I can see you, anyway."

"What do you see in there?" Alex asked.

"Is there anything gross?" Missy inquired. "I don't want to mess up my hair on this." Paul gave her a sideways glance of disapproval. She giggled.

"No, nothing gross," the voice came back. "It's just, well..."

"What?" Valerie wondered aloud, leaning into Paul's ComWatch.

"It's hard to see even with my I-Glasses. It's dark."

"How dark?" Alex implored, gulping. *I wish I'd never found this place,* he thought. He warmed up his thoughts by envisioning tomorrow's birthday cake and colorful gifts. They'd be a day late, but better late than—

"Wait! I see something." The Superkids froze like ice skaters suddenly hearing a crack in the ice. They waited for her to elaborate. Rapper knelt on the ground and peered into the dark.

"I can't see anything," he muttered.

"There's writing on the *pffft,*" Commander Kellie continued.

"What's a *pffft?*" Alex asked, wide-eyed. Missy giggled again, but it sounded like a nervous giggle.

"*Pffft* is what you hear when the ComWatch charges are low," Rapper explained, still down on all fours. "We'll have to fix that later."

"You're cutting out," Paul reported back to Commander Kellie matter-of-factly. Alex hoped the ComWatch charges would last. With a questioning look, Paul asked, "You said you see writing?"

"What?" the commander asked. "You're cutting out. The ComWa-*pffft* break-*pffft* up." Paul thumped the ComWatch with his finger.

"What is it you see?" Paul asked again.

"Here's *pffft*-thing *pffft*-rious."

"You see something *serious?*" Paul questioned, attempting to make sense of the racket. He was squinting at the watch face, even though there was nothing on it. Missy bit her lip and twisted a lock of her lengthy, blond hair with her index finger as she looked over Paul's shoulder. Valerie bent down and joined Rapper, groping to see into the blackness. Alex didn't move. His hands felt warm and tingly. *I will not be afraid for God is with me,* he quietly recited over and over to himself, quoting Joshua 1:9.

"No...*pffft* mysteri-*pffft*."

"Mysterious," Missy said, completing Commander Kellie's sentence. "She sees something mysterious."

Paul nodded. "What is it?" he demanded. "Maybe we should come in."

"Wait...*pffft*-s some kind of presence in here."

Alex froze. "A *presence?*" he declared. "She means *God's* presence, right?" Paul looked at Alex.

"A *presence?*" Paul repeated into the ComWatch's transmitter. There was a long pause, then the ComWatch spit up the words, **"CONNECTION LOST."** Paul thumped the device again. "Commander Kellie? Are you there?"

The only response was silence.

"Commander Kellie!" Rapper and Valerie yelled into the hole, sweeping their flashlight beams into the darkness beyond. Alex leaned against the rough wall across from the hole, with his left hand pressed against his forehead. He was feeling hot. Missy grabbed Paul's wrist, pulling the ComWatch toward her. "What'd you do with her?" she shrieked at Paul. Then she shouted into the ComWatch, "Commander Kellie—are you there?"

"What did *I* do with her?" Paul argued, shaking her off. "Nothing! One minute she was there, the next minute she vanished!"

"We have to go in after her," Rapper concluded, still peering into the hole.

Missy shook her head. "That's nuts! We need to go tell another commander about this."

"She said there was a *presence* in there," Alex said, feeling the blood run out of his face. "What could it be?"

"I'm going in," Rapper insisted, pulling the goggles off his head with one hand and unsnapping his flashlight from his belt with another. Valerie grabbed his shirt.

"You're not going in, Robert, it's too dangerous."

"Commander Kellie needs us. I'm going in. And I told you not to call me Robert."

"Whoo-whoo!" Missy chided. "Touchy, aren't we?" Robert Rapfield was Rapper's real name, but ever since he was old enough to talk, everyone called him "Rapper," because he loved to rap. Valerie was the only exception. For some reason unknown to Alex, once in a while she preferred to call him by his real name. But even so, because of his protests, she rarely did.

"There's no time for this," Paul ordered. "But Val's right. You shouldn't go in. We need to get help."

Alex perceived that Rapper knew better than to argue with Paul. After all, Commander Kellie had put him in charge. From the first day Alex had met Paul, he saw the influential way Paul had with people. If anyone could get them out of a jam, he could.

A moment later, Paul ordered Missy and Rapper to leave with him to find another commander. He wanted Valerie and Alex to stay by the hole in case they heard something from Commander Kellie. Techno stayed, too.

▲ ▲ ▲

"I can't believe this happened on my birthday," Alex said to Valerie once the others were gone. He paced the floor.

Valerie finished programming her ComWatch to receive transmissions from the commander. It flashed a message reading, **"UNABLE TO CONNECT,"** but Valerie left it on anyway. She looked into the hole, hoping to see some kind of movement, but it was too dark. Then she stood up and pulled out a pocket-sized Bible. She found the verse she was looking for—Colossians 3:15—and pointed it out to Alex. "Let the peace of Christ rule in your hearts," Valerie read. Then she closed her Bible and put it back in her pocket. "Don't be afraid, Alex. God's presence is right here with us...and it's the most powerful presence of all."

Alex nodded. That's one thing he admired a lot about Valerie. She believed anything the Bible said without wavering. Her faith in the Lord was very strong. Alex often found himself talking to Valerie for encouragement. Her soft, brown eyes twinkled.

Thump-thump-thump-thump! Paul, Missy and Rapper ran by, heading in the opposite direction from which they'd left at first. Visions of *The Three Stooges*™ ran through Alex's head. Valerie shook her own.

"This is going to take each of us doing our part," she continued. "Let's be sure to be ready with our gifts."

"Gifts?"

"Yeah. God has given us each special abilities...and we'll need them all to come through in victory."

Alex smiled weakly, but wasn't sure how to respond. Sure, it was easy for her to "be ready with her gifts," because she—like the other Superkids—had so many abilities. Her faith in God was firm, like a deeply rooted tree. She wanted to be a commander. *And* she was a great pilot. *But here I am,* Alex thought, *nervous and not sure what to do next!*

Valerie's button nose wrinkled. "God can use you, Alex. All you have to do is be available."

"Be available to do what? I can't do much." He sat down beside her.

Valerie was obviously shocked at his words. "Are you kidding? God can use you if you're simply available to do *anything* for Him." She pointed at him in a way that reminded him of Commander Kellie. "You have quite a bit of talent stuffed inside there. I'm sure of it."

Thump-thump-thump-thump! Paul, Missy and Rapper came running back. This time they stopped.

"That was fast," Valerie observed.

"You haven't heard or seen anything?" Paul asked.

"Nope," Alex answered, checking out Valerie's ComWatch. "Is help coming?"

"Nope," Missy imitated Alex's word. "We can't get out of either of the two doors that lead into this hallway. We electronically sealed both when we entered so that no one would come in while we were working with the explosives."

"Well, who has the passcode?" Valerie asked.

"Commander Kellie," Paul said with a huff.

It took a moment for it to register. "You mean we're *locked* in here?" Alex shot the question at no one in particular.

"Well, we have the *presence* on the other side of this hole to keep us company," Missy said jokingly. But nobody laughed. They all just stood silently for a moment.

Alex broke the silence with an idea. "Hey, why don't we see if we can reach someone outside with our ComWatches?" He tapped a couple buttons on his own, but the familiar **"UNABLE TO CONNECT"** message flashed on the small, flat screen.

Techno's domed head lit up with blue lines which formed a crude map of the old NME building. "It's the walls," he computed. "They're made of some kind of thick metal alloy that diffuses our communication waves."

"NME probably built them like that to keep others from tapping in to their plans," Alex reasoned.

"OK, but how could we talk with Commander Kellie then?" Rapper wondered. "We were using communication waves while talking to her..."

"Yeah," Paul answered. "But there's a hole in the wall to let the waves through to her." Rapper nodded. Techno turned off the map.

"Then we'll have to go in," Rapper said.

The words echoed like a thundering storm inside Alex's head—*We'll have to go in.* Alex gulped audibly.

"Well, as the oldest, Commander Kellie put me in charge," Paul said. "I'll go in after her." No one objected. Paul tapped his ComWatch and looked at Valerie. "Keep in touch," he said. "If I find her, I'll let you know."

"What do you mean, *'if'* you find her?" Missy stammered.

"He means, 'when' he finds her," Valerie corrected. Paul nodded and ran his long fingers through his wavy, blond hair. It tumbled back into place.

"I think we should pray first," Valerie said, reaching out toward Rapper with one hand and Missy with the other. Missy looked at Paul.

"I can't hold his hand. Boys got cooties."

Paul's eyebrows jumped up. "Coo—*what?* Missy!"

She tipped her head. "Oh, I'm just trying to lighten the mood."

"Well, you're not helping," Valerie said, suppressing a chuckle. "We need to pray." Her conviction was so strong that everyone agreed. In unison, each Superkid found another's hand and they formed a small circle. Alex closed his eyes after everyone else did. The room was silent for a moment.

"Who's going to pray?" Missy asked, snapping her head up impatiently.

Paul raised his head and caught Missy's gaze. "Why don't *you* pray, Missy." Missy pushed her bottom lip out with her tongue and dropped her head. Her feet shuffled on the floor and then she began.

"God," she prayed, "I pray You'll forgive Paul for being so direct with me." Alex opened his eyes and saw Paul raise his head and open one eye in protest.

"And I pray that You'll help us find Commander Kellie's body..." Rapper's head popped up.

"And if Techno's head is too big to help us in the future, please help us find a good recycling program for him..." Techno spun his metallic eye sockets around to face Missy.

"And, um, I also pray that my friends would develop a good sense of humor." Valerie's head shot up and she glared at Missy.

"Thank You for answering all these prayers, God. Amen." Missy looked up with a warm smile and then jumped when she saw all 10 eyes staring at her.

"Missy, prayer is serious." Valerie was firm. Missy's smile faded and a moment passed as she nodded apologetically.

Valerie let out a cool breath. "I'll pray." She dropped her head. Alex watched each head go down again and then bowed his own.

"Father God, we come before You now in the mighty Name of Jesus and ask for Your guidance and protection. Today we choose to walk by faith and not by what we see. We don't know what kind of unknown presence is behind this hole, but we do know that *Your* presence is with us wherever we go. So now we believe, like it says in Your Word in Psalm 91:11, that Your angels are in charge of us, watching over us wherever we go. And we believe that You will give us the wisdom to rescue Commander Kellie and to solve this mystery. Thank You for Your anointing in us. We rely on it today. We also pray for Your same powerful protection for Commander Kellie. Lord, be with her now. We trust in You and praise You for the answer. In Jesus' Name. Amen."

"Amen," Paul repeated. "Thank you, Valerie."

"What about me?" Missy asked.

"You can thank Valerie, too, if you like," Paul responded.

"I'm sorry, guys. I was just trying to lighten things up. I guess I got carried away."

"I believe in having fun," Paul said. "But I'm about to enter this hole. And I hope that when I do, you take it seriously and don't start wondering if you'll ever find my body."

The look in Missy's eyes said her apology was sincere.

"Yo!" Rapper shouted. "Let's not waste any more time. I'm hungry."

Everyone looked at Rapper, a little surprised at the outburst.

"How can you think of food at a time like this?" Alex asked.

"It's just a figure of speech," Rapper explained. "'I'm hungry' is rap for, uh, 'Let's get this party moving.'" He smiled. "You know?"

Paul knelt down in front of the dark hole near the floor. Standing behind him, Alex could feel warm air blowing in from the dark expanse beyond. He wondered again what could possibly be back there.

Perhaps it was nothing. Maybe the ComWatches just needed to be charged and that's why they had lost contact with Commander Kellie. Alex reasoned that she could be exploring the large room and just hadn't returned yet.

But then why didn't she answer when they called? Did she hurt herself? Could she have tripped over something in the dark and been knocked unconscious? That sounded reasonable...but she said there was some kind of mysterious presence in the room. And there was some writing somewhere...

Paul put his hand inside the hole and felt around the back. "Well, it feels like a normal wall," he reported, with a half smile.

"Eww!" Missy cried, wincing. "How can you even put your hand in there not knowing what's on the other side."

"Well, I'm getting ready to put my whole self in here in just a minute. I figure this is the best way to get ready.

Kind of like feeling pool water with your toes before you jump in."

Yeah, Alex thought, *but when you go into pools, you come back out.*

"Techno," Paul addressed the robot. "Can you scan through this hole and see what's on the other side again?" Techno wheeped and whirred for a moment. He rolled as close as he could get without blocking the hole with his lower body.

"I read oxygen and dust like before," Techno reported. After a brief pause he choked out a beep. "Wait! There's something else in there that I didn't catch the first time!"

The Superkids waited in anticipation as Techno finished his analysis. He bleeped and buzzed some more as his computer database came up with some answers.

"What is it?" Alex asked the robot. "What's back there?"

Alex put a lot of trust in Techno's abilities. When Alex first arrived at Superkid Academy, his first friend was this machine of metal and electronic parts. It's not that no one wanted to be Alex's friend, it's just that Alex found it easy to relate to the robot. Maybe it was because he loved computers and technology or maybe it was because Techno wasn't like everyone else...and that's how Alex felt sometimes.

They were both about the same height, and even though Techno was a computer, sometimes he, like Alex, had trouble communicating. So their friendship began. Now, over the past couple years, Alex had gained many more friends, especially his four Blue Squad companions. But Techno would always be near the top of his list... even if he wasn't human.

Alex knew this was one of those times when Techno's unique abilities could come into play and really help the others. His confidence in what Techno was designed to do was soaring.

Techno suddenly stopped whirring.

"I sense a human in there. Alive and breathing."

"Commander Kellie," Paul said to the four other Superkids gathered around Techno.

"So she's all right," Missy said. She let out a sigh of relief.

"Wait—there's still something else," Techno reported. "But it will take me awhile to figure out what it is... I don't think I've run into this before." Everyone's eyes turned to Techno.

"Great," Rapper said with his thumb up. "So Commander Kellie is in there and all right, but there's something else, too. Hey, Paul, if we wait a moment, we'll know what the mysterious presence is and we might be able to beat this thing, huh?"

"I just knew everything would turn out all right," Missy cooed.

"Isn't that right, Paul?" Rapper asked, looking around him.

"I'm so glad this is almost over!" Missy cheered.

"Hey, guys..." Rapper was darting his brown eyes all around the room. "Where's Paul?"

"Oh, no!" Missy dropped down on the floor and peered into the hole. "Do you think he was...taken?"

"Do you think *who* was taken?" came a voice from behind the hole.

"Paul," Missy continued. "Do you think Paul was taken into the hole by some horrible presence?"

"I don't think so," the voice came back. "I think he probably entered it of his own free will when he heard Commander Kellie was still in there, alive and well."

"Do you really think he's...*Paul? Is that you?"

Valerie giggled at the joke. Missy blushed. "That's not funny, Paul." She slapped the wall above the hole. Granules of dust trickled down like snowflakes.

"I'm sorry," Paul said from the other side. "It was just too easy."

Valerie and Rapper joined Missy down at the entrance. A little hesitant, Alex knelt down, too.

"You know, Techno says there's something else in there," Alex warned. "And it will be harder for you to see—Commander Kellie had our only pair of I-Glasses."

Paul didn't respond, but instead spat out a few orders. "I'm going to go looking around, and I'll keep in touch through Val's ComWatch. But just to be safe, I'll also come back here every two minutes and report in." The Superkids nodded their heads. "If, for some reason, I don't come back, then Val's in charge." Missy looked like she was going to protest for a moment, but then conceded. Alex knew that despite their differences, Missy and Valerie had been close friends a long time and trusted each other greatly.

"I imagine Commander Kellie has just tripped and been knocked out and I'll have her out of here in a sec. If you can, try to follow my flashlight so you always know where I am. Got it?"

Heads nodded. Valerie verbalized that his instructions were understood and switched her watch to link up with her leader's. Paul's hand appeared from out of the hole and each Superkid grabbed it in unison. The stack of hands looked like a crude clay sculpture. Alex's hand was the darkest, on top, holding on to Rapper's hand. His hand was on top of Valerie's naturally tanned hand and she held on to Missy's stark-white hand. Missy held on to Paul's hand. They were a unified team; they needed to be.

Alex always felt moments like these were bittersweet. He loved feeling the camaraderie, but despised knowing that someone could potentially be entering danger.

A moment later, as each Superkid released their hand from the stack, Paul's hand drifted into the void beyond.

▲ ▲ ▲

Though it seemed like an eternity, less than two minutes later Paul's hand reappeared at the hole. He hadn't talked much through the ComWatches, and he surprised everyone when he suddenly showed up.

"Hey, guys!" he shouted. Every one of the remaining Superkids jumped back. Alex even thought he saw Techno roll back a bit.

"Paul!" Valerie exclaimed. "Did you find any clues?"

"Not yet." Paul sounded disappointed. "I'm still looking. There's stuff everywhere. You would not believe the junk in this place."

"What should we do?" Alex asked.

"Well, let me look around more. Just follow my flashlight beam again."

"It's too dark in there, Paul," Valerie protested. "Even with your beam on its highest intensity, last time we couldn't follow it for very long and your voice became garbled in the ComWatch. Maybe you went too far. Can you stay more in view?"

Paul's hand showed a thumbs up. "Can do," he said. "I'll try to stay closer this time."

▲ ▲ ▲

The next time in, the Superkids were able to track Paul's flashlight beam and talk to him about the messy room for nearly the full two minutes he was exploring. Seeing the light and hearing his voice was a comfort to Alex, who just wanted to get Commander Kellie out and the whole mess to be over.

Paul returned and stuck his hand out of the hole again to signal his arrival. Alex knew he could have come out farther, but to bend through would be somewhat of a pain, so he just thrust his hand into the room to let everyone know he had returned. At times, they could see a piece of his shoe or pant leg, but for the most part, it was so dark inside the hole that even those details were concealed.

"So?" Missy asked impatiently.

"Well, I found a lot more junk, but no sign of Commander Kellie. I need to go farther into the room. I think I saw some of the writing she saw, but it's large and I couldn't make it all out in the dark without getting closer. I'll just have to go in deeper."

"Paul, are you sure you want to do this?" Missy's concern was evident. "If you go farther, we may lose all communication with you."

Paul's hand moved from side to side. "Don't worry," came the corresponding words, "I'll be back again in two minutes."

Two minutes came and went...and Paul's hand didn't appear again. Alex, like the rest, was waiting for those familiar fingers to pop into the light and give a cheery hello—like a sock puppet jumping up from behind a stage. But the darkness stayed dark. About four minutes had passed since they had last seen the dancing of Paul's flashlight beam or heard the assurance of his voice. They waited in silence.

Alex found it hard to believe that it had only been an hour since Commander Kellie first went into the hole and told them about the presence—and then vanished. Techno was sure he detected her, and now Paul, too, but Alex couldn't see either one from where he sat. He was directly across from the hole and Missy was at his right, fiddling with some strands of her blond hair. On his left sat Rapper and Valerie, both with question marks on their faces, staring at Valerie's ComWatch. It was now reading, **"CONNECTION LOST."** Rapper's eyebrows went up and down in acknowledgment when Alex caught his eye.

Then another minute passed.

Then another.

And another.

"It has been 10 minutes," Techno reported. Alex looked at each of the Superkids with him and sighed.

"He's gone, too, isn't he?" he whispered, looking at Valerie for the answer.

"I think that's safe to assume," Rapper said, squeezing the bridge of his nose with the fingertips of both hands.

Missy leaned over and yelled into the crawl way, "Paul Temp, you'd better get out here now or you're gonna get it!"

No answer came.

"Great," Missy said flatly.

"I don't think he's 'gone,'" Valerie finally said, taking charge and standing up. "I think he's not answering." She pushed some buttons on her ComWatch and then addressed Techno. "What do you detect?"

"Same as before, but with an added human. Both Commander Kellie and Paul are alive."

"Can you tell where in the room they are?" Valerie asked point-blank.

"I'm not equipped for finding direct location. But I do have on file 2,439 different recipes incorporating Jell-O...just so you know for future reference."

Valerie smiled at Techno's informative wit. "Thanks, but I'll stick with what I already know."

"OK, let's think." Valerie began to pace. Her soft, dark hair bounced from its resting position on her shoulders. Alex stood up to show his support. Valerie began to think out loud. "We're locked in the hall, so we can't get help. Commander Kellie and Paul have vanished, possibly due to some mysterious presence, but more likely because they've tripped and need our help. Obviously, the only thing we can do is keep trying."

Missy jumped up. "You're not suggesting more of us go in there?"

"C'mon, Missy, you know Valerie's right. We don't have a choice," Rapper said.

"Maybe we should try a new strategy," Alex suggested.

"Exactly." Valerie smiled and nodded. "I think I know just what to do."

"What?" Missy asked Valerie.

"I'm going to go in there," Valerie started.

"Good idea," Rapper agreed.

"And *you're* coming with me," Valerie continued, grabbing Rapper's arm and pulling him up off the floor.

"Bad idea," Rapper disagreed, struggling to sit back down—but Missy was holding him up by his other arm. In a swift movement, she pulled his left arm behind his back.

"Ow!" he cried, wincing.

"Say you'll do it!" Missy pushed. "Say you'll do it!"

"OK! OK!" Rapper conceded. *"You'll* do it."

Missy pushed on his arm, twisting it back harder. "Rapper!"

"OK! *I'll* do it!" Missy let go and Rapper grabbed his arm and massaged it. "Ashton," he said, calling Missy by her last name, "where'd you learn to do that?"

"That's how I let my dad know what I want for Christmas," she answered, blowing on her fingernails. Alex laughed for the first time since they entered the hallway.

Valerie proceeded to lay out the plan. She explained that both she and Rapper would enter the hole, but stay back-to-back. That way, they could better avoid trouble by watching each other's back. Missy muttered something about being thankful that they had all brought working flashlights for the excursion.

"Well, this is the best idea yet," Rapper admitted.

"But what about the mysterious presence?" Alex wondered.

Valerie shook her head and shrugged her shoulders. "I really don't think that's a logical explanation. I don't believe in monsters and I don't believe in a mysterious presence. But even if there were one, with us going in back-to-back, it'll be pretty hard to sneak up on us."

Not wanting to argue, Alex yielded...but he wasn't as convinced as Valerie that nothing was in there.

Valerie and Rapper both checked their flashlights with a tap on their control panels and then looked at Missy and Alex.

"Worst case scenario," Valerie stated, "if we don't come back, Missy...you're the captain."

Alex felt a rush of relief. He didn't want to be in charge. Especially if Missy would have to follow his orders. He knew that would work out about as well as trying to light a wet match.

Alex didn't think Missy was mean or rebellious— she was just headstrong. If she thought something should be done a different way than you, she didn't mind saying so. And Alex didn't like confrontation.

On the other hand, he really had learned a lot from Missy, though he'd probably never let it be known. Her outgoing personality and enthusiasm for life were contagious. And though sometimes her attitude in a situation was against the grain—like her joking earlier— she usually knew when enough was enough. And more than anything, when she gave you a compliment she could make you feel extremely good about yourself...because when she said she liked something about you, you knew she meant it.

You can always take Missy at face value, Alex thought.

"Ready, Robert—er, Rapper?" Valerie winced at her mistake. Rapper just rolled his eyes and nodded a "yes." They both turned on their flashlights and, back-to-back, bent down and proceeded to enter into the darkness.

"I know that there should be nothin' to it—but the fact of the matter is, I just can't do it!" Rapper rapped and jumped back out of the hole.

Alex always got a kick out of Rapper putting words together in such a witty way. But it was rapping that also gave Rapper's nervousness away. Some people's knees shake, others get butterflies in their stomach or a sweaty upper lip. But Rapper just starts rapping.

On the contrary, one thing Alex really admired Rapper for was his courage. It was this quality that made him, like Valerie, one of the Academy's best pilots. And it was also this quality that kept him from being self-conscious around new acquaintances. Alex liked his style. It was uniquely...Rapper.

"Don't be nervous," Alex said reassuringly. Missy opened her mouth with a smirk, like she was going to crack a joke, but then thought better of it. Instead she just put her hands on Rapper's shoulders and looked him square in the eye.

"Rapper, none of us wants to go in there," she reassured him. "But there's no other way around this. We're locked in, our friends are missing and we need your help. Remember Psalm 23:4—'Even though I walk through the valley of the shadow of death, I will fear no evil, for you are with me.'"

Rapper bit his lip and looked straight into Missy's eyes intently.

Rapper seemed to get the idea. He nodded again and said a weak, "OK. You're right. If God is for us, who can be against us?"

"Romans 8:31," Techno stated, acknowledging the scripture.

Rapper and Valerie scrunched down to enter the hole again. Inch-by-dreadful-inch they moved in. As they entered, Alex heard Rapper rap, "Here we go, Val—it's not much fun. But one thing's for sure...it's gotta be done."

As they descended into the hidden room, Alex felt a tightening in his stomach—just like when Commander Kellie had entered for the first time. For some reason, the others didn't seem as jolted by the strenuous circumstances as he did. Sure, Rapper seemed nervous and Missy wasn't as happy as she'd been when they first arrived, but they were all handling this better than Alex. Even Valerie, who Alex knew wasn't fond of the dark, was bearing up and going in without a word of protest.

Nonetheless, Alex felt justified in his wariness. First Commander Kellie vanished, then Paul disappeared...and now Valerie and Rapper were entering the same abyss.

Sure, Valerie thought that Commander Kellie and Paul had both simply tripped or something...but what if there was a mysterious presence back there? That's what the commander had said, wasn't it? If only there were some other way...

But Alex knew there wasn't. The only way out of this trap was to go boldly into the darkness and confront the problem. They couldn't just run away from it. The doors on the outside were locked and some of their group could be hurt. They had to put their faith in God, believing that He would help them find the key so they could all walk out to freedom together. It wasn't an easy solution, but it seemed to be the sole solution. *If only there were another way,* Alex thought again. *If only…*

Alex and Missy got down on all fours and peered into the hole. For just a second, Alex thought he saw Rapper, but he couldn't be sure. He could still see their sweeping flashlight beams though, and their voices could be heard from Missy's ComWatch.

"What'd you say?" Missy asked. She tucked her long, straight, blond hair behind her right ear. The ComWatch was crackling madly. "I can barely understand them," she said to Alex. She turned the volume down on the ComWatch and leaned into the hole. With all the crackling from the ComWatch, it seemed like they could hear more just by listening through the hole. Alex leaned closer also, but kept his legs arched just in case he needed to get away from the hole quickly.

"Something about a…stream?" Alex cocked his head. "That doesn't make any sense."

"Shhh…listen." Missy held her left hand up in the air like she was surrendering to an enemy. Her right hand was supporting her as she leaned in.

As Alex listened he thought he heard Valerie say something about something being beautiful…was that…did Rapper just snicker? This was too strange. Then for a lengthy period there was silence.

Alex looked over at Missy and saw her eyes close for a long moment. Her lips looked like they were whispering a quick prayer. Her prayerful state brought brief comfort to Alex, but the silence from Rapper and Valerie brought even more discomfort. Alex felt his body lighten and he felt queasy. He could hear his own heartbeat in his ears…He felt as though he was about to faint…

"Hellllllooooo!"

Alex jolted to his feet just before he went under. Little silver stars danced around his head as the room spun. A small smile appeared on his face as he imagined that he had just woken up from a long nightmare. He delighted in seeing the light around him. And there was his computer friend, Techno. And there was Missy. And there was…the hole. The smile left Alex's face. He steadied himself.

"I think I stood up too fast," he said.

"Hellllllooooo? Anybody there?"

"Missy, the ComWatch!" Alex pointed to her watch. She turned up the volume. They were coming through loud and clear now.

"What'd you find?" Alex hoped for good news.

"Nothing. We haven't found the commander yet," Rapper replied. "And we haven't seen Paul either."

Missy let out a sigh and Alex felt relieved that at least Rapper and Valerie were all right. And somehow, hearing their voices again made Alex feel one step closer to solving the mystery.

"Have they seen anything else?" Alex questioned.

"Have you seen anything else?" Missy repeated into the ComWatch.

"Well, it's hard to say…" Rapper's voice trailed off.

"I thought I heard you say something about a stream," Alex mentioned quizzically. Missy added, "Yeah, and I think I heard Val say something was beautiful. What was she talking about?"

Rapper's voice garbled through the communicator again. "Yeah, well, we have seen some interesting things…. We'll have to come back and tell you about them. It's too hard to talk into the ComWatch, walk back-to-back and hold a flashlight all at once."

"I could do it," Missy whispered to Alex.

"That's because you're such an expert at talking," Rapper quipped. Missy blushed. She obviously didn't think he had heard her comment.

"OK, well, we're going to ret—"

BAM! CRASH! SPLASH! The ComWatch went silent.

▲　▲　▲

For five minutes, according to Techno, Alex and Missy tried to get Rapper to answer their call. But there was no response. Then suddenly his voice sounded, much to their relief.

"I'm soaked," is what he said.

"Yes!" Missy chirped, happy to hear her friend's voice again. Alex wiped some beads of perspiration from the back of his neck. "What happened?" he asked.

"I am *drenched*," Rapper replied. Missy looked confused.

"I bet he fell into the stream," Alex reasoned.

"It's a *room*," Missy argued. "How can there be a stream in there?" Alex didn't have an explanation. Nothing seemed to add up.

"I told you I couldn't talk and walk at the same time," Rapper said. "Look, we're coming *pffft*."

"Great, the watches are acting up again," Missy said, standing up and stretching her legs. "You're cutting out," she shouted into the ComWatch. Silence prevailed momentarily, then Rapper's voice came through loud and clear.

"OK. It's not a low charge, like we thought. The problem is when I go back behind some of this junk. Apparently it blocks our communication from getting through—that's why we're clear, then garbled, then clear again. We've been weaving around."

"So don't go so far!" Missy shouted enthusiastically, squeezing her fists tightly.

"No, Val wants to go deeper. Don't you see?! This will bring us closer to the answer. Commander Kellie cut out just before she disappeared. And we lost Paul when he went exploring farther than we could see. If we go on, we may just find them."

Valerie's voice came on. "Don't worry, Superkids. We're together, and remember the Superkid Manual says in Psalm 61:3 that God is our protection—He's a strong tower against our enemies. We'll be all right."

Rapper's voice returned a few seconds later. "Here we go...*pffft* not much different he-*pffft*."

"I don't like this," Alex whispered. Missy knelt back down and looked into the hole.

"Now here *is* some-*pffft* mysterious...I've got to dry *pffft*...Val, what do you make of...*pffft*...pres-*pffft*... Val?...*pffft*...Val?...*pffft*..*pffft*...Oh, n—"

"CONNECTION LOST."

"This is ridiculous," Missy spat with a spark of anger. "Where are they vanishing to? Is this some kind of cruel NME joke?"

Alex was dumbfounded. He was alone with Hypergirl and a robot sporting Jell-O recipes—no one else was left to save the day. Why did he have to find this hidden room in the first place? Why didn't he try to make everyone take this as serious as he did? They didn't believe in a mysterious presence...but Alex did.

Missy took off her jacket. Then her shoes. Alex sent a sideways glance her way. Then she removed her belt. *It's official,* Alex thought, s*he has gone nuts.*

"Now's not the time to go swimming," Alex said as she began to pull at her socks. She stopped and looked at him like a hungry cat looks at a mouse.

"Give me your jacket," Missy ordered.

You're in charge, he thought. He pulled off his royal blue Academy wear. Alex winced when she pulled her socks all the way off.

"Missy..."

She looked at him again, determined. He was half expecting laser bolts to shoot out of her eyes. Alex waved his hand in front of his nose. "Maybe you'd better keep your socks on." He couldn't figure out what in the world she was doing.

"I need your goggles, too," she said, holding out her hand toward him. Shrugging, he pulled them from around his neck. She grabbed them enthusiastically and with a *snap!* she yanked off the thick rubber band that had snugly held them on Alex's head. She did the same with her own pair.

"Are you sure you should—"

"OK. Now give me your shoes, socks and anything else you have that isn't absolutely necessary."

Alex untied his shoes and pulled them off. A cooling sensation hit his feet. He lifted his shoes into the air. "Actually, these are kind of necessary where I come from." Missy ignored him. Alex shook his head and then pulled off his socks and his belt, too. "Missy, maybe you should tell me what—"

"Help me with this," she interrupted. Alex wasn't about to argue. Following her lead, he began to tie each piece of clothing together. One by one, the articles began to form a long, crude connection. A belt connected to a shoelace, connected to a thick rubber band, connected to a couple of socks, connected to another shoelace, a couple more socks, and another thick rubber band. Missy tied the end of the last rubber band to Alex's jacket sleeve. Then, she zipped the left half of Alex's jacket up with the right half of her own—forming a funny-looking, extra-big jacket. Finally, she took the other belt and set one of the belt holes in between a snap and its connection on her coat sleeve. Unhooking her ComWatch, Missy shoved it through the belt's buckle and then refastened it. She motioned to the other end of the line of clothes.

"You hold on to that shoelace," she said. "I'm going in." Alex thought he misunderstood her.

"Huh?"

"I'm going in," she restated, "and you're staying here as my safeguard. You hold one end and I'll hold on to the other. As long as you don't let go, you'll know just where to find me if something happens."

"I don't like this plan." Alex imagined himself having to enter the dark hole to find Missy.

"Alex, I'm counting on you," she said sternly. "If you feel me stop moving, you need to follow this rope in and get me. I don't want to end up stuck in there like...all our friends."

Alex nodded. Not because he wanted to, but because he knew he had to. Missy wasted no time. She double-checked all the clothes' connections, punched on her flashlight and bent down to enter the darkness.

"Wait!" cried Techno just before Missy disappeared. "I've got it!"

Missy stopped and whirled around. "You've got what?"

"I told you earlier that I sensed something else in there—remember?" Techno was wharpling zestful electric beeps.

"I remember," Alex said, moving toward the robot.

"Well, I finally figured out what it is!"

"What is it?" Alex asked anxiously. "What's in there?"

"Well," Techno computed. "I sense five items containing cells. Four are human."

"Commander Kellie, Paul, Rapper and Val," Missy reasoned.

"That's correct," Techno agreed.

"So what else do you detect?" Missy inquired.

"A huge…" Alex hung on every word. "Healthy…" Missy was leaning in. "Herbaceous perennial of the genus Fragaria."

Missy covered her mouth as her face turned pale. "That sounds awful!" she cried through cupped hands.

Alex took two steps back and felt like lying down.

"Just tell me this, Techno," Missy said, breathing heavily. "Don't hold anything back. Tell me…could it eat humans?"

"Not unless it's an especially harmful form of strawberry," Techno replied.

Missy blinked noticeably.

"What did you say?" she asked.

"Not unless it's—"

"After that."

"I didn't say anything after that. You did."

"No. You said it was a form of something."

"A harmful form of strawberry," Techno said. "But I doubt that's it. I've never known anyone to be harmed by a strawberry. Well, not intentionally anyway."

Missy slugged Techno so hard on his glass dome he nearly fell over. "Are you telling me the only other thing you sense in there is a *strawberry?!?*"

"Well, you asked…"

"Oh—my goodness! Ugh! Techno! I can't believe you just sat there and told me it's some horrendous, prowling—whatever you said—genius fang-monster!"

"That's 'herbaceous perennial of the genus Fragaria.' It's the scientific term for 'strawberry.'"

Missy cooled down and let out a long breath. Alex thought she looked like she was counting to 10 to help put things in perspective. He made a mental note to talk to Techno about his scientific explanations. But right now, Alex was just glad it wasn't something really bad.

"I'm not wasting any more time," Missy said finally. "I'm going in."

"Missy, are you sure?" Alex warned.

"You heard him," she retorted, placing her hands on her hips. "There's nothing in there but four humans and a big strawberry. Obviously, they've just been knocked out or become caught in some kind of wild NME maze. It's no big deal."

Alex dropped his head.

"Look." She sounded more sympathetic. "I'm still going to be hooked to the clothes line so you can find me. I won't use the ComWatch since it only works so far. I'll just talk as loud as I can the whole time so you can know I'm all right even if you can't see my flashlight, OK?"

Alex nodded and gathered his courage. Then he smiled. "OK. I guess the possibility of a strawberry eating you is pretty small anyway."

▲ ▲ ▲

Missy entered the hole, with the clothes trail firmly attached to her ComWatch. Since the line was so heavy, rather than wear the watch, she held on to it. If she had tried wearing it, more than likely it would have popped right off with the weight anyway.

As promised, she entered the hole talking loudly and didn't stop. It was comforting for Alex to hear her voice, even though he was in the hall alone with Techno.

"OK, I'm walking…I'm walking…" she was saying. Alex had to giggle a little at the irony. After all, if anyone could talk nonstop, Missy could. And now she had to.

"And it's really dark in here…and this 'clothes rope' sounded like a good idea, but it's really heavy…and I don't see any stream…and I don't see any writing yet… and there's nothing really beautiful about this place…at least not on the floor…and there's a lot of junk sitting around…"

Alex looked up at Techno. He whirled his domed head in a complete circle.

"And I don't see any monster strawberries…and I'm glad about that…and I'm gonna need a new coat after mine has been dragged all over this dirty floor…and my feet are getting cold…and oh! I need to paint my toenails…"

Alex wrapped the shoelace he was holding on to around the back of his hand. The clothesline was quickly getting taut.

"And have you ever heard the joke about the guy who owned a broken mirror? No? Well, that's all right. It's not worth reflecting on...and whoa! The line's tight. I'll go another way..."

Alex felt her switch direction as he held the shoelace.

"And you know, I never got my mail today. I think I'll do that if I'm not eaten by a herbaceous, er, whatever..."

"Herbaceous perennial of the genus Fragaria," Techno offered. Alex smiled.

"And...and...and...Where is everyone? Commander Kellie? Paul? Valerie? Rap...er...Robert? *Robert?*" she sang.

"You're supposed to be staying *out* of trouble, remember?!" Alex shouted into the hole. Missy paused for a moment.

"Oops, it just slipped out," she explained, without convincing Alex. "Let's see...what to talk about...knock, knock...hey! Knock! Knock!"

Alex suddenly realized she was addressing him. "Uh, who's there?" he shouted back.

"Banana!" Missy sang.

"Banana, who?" Alex yelled back.

"Knock, knock!"

Alex paused for a moment. "You already said that!"

"I said, 'Knock, knock!'"

Alex gave in. "Who's there?"

"Banana!"

"Banana, who?"

"Knock, knock!"

"Who's there?"

"Banana!"

"Banana, *who?*" Alex yelled even louder.

"Knock, knock!"

"Who's there?"

"Orange!"

Alex rolled his eyes. He replied, "Orange, who?"

Silence.

"Orange, who?" he hollered again.

Without warning, the line of clothes thumped to the ground like a huge stuffed animal falling from the sky. Then he heard a sudden scream that was cut surprisingly short.

Frantically, Alex wrapped the shoestring he held around Techno's metal claw-like hand. He ordered Techno to slowly roll backward down the hall, to pull Missy out. He didn't want to drag her along the floor, but he really didn't want to enter the hole himself— because if he was taken, they would *all* be lost forever.

He didn't know if his companions had been the victims of a mysterious presence or captured by a man-eating strawberry—but he didn't want to find out. He just wanted to get Missy out. If he did, maybe she could tell him something.

Like a fisherman reeling in the taut line of a prize catch, Techno slowly rolled backward down the hall. The shoestring became a belt and the belt became a thick rubber band. The rope was surprisingly light, Alex thought, to have a person holding on to the end. Within minutes, Techno was far down the hallway. Out from the darkness came Alex's jacket, attached to Missy's jacket. Then came the belt. Alex was peering in to see if Missy was still holding on. It was too dark to see...but then with a clink-clink-clink, her ComWatch, affixed to the end of her belt, came bouncing out.

There was no sign of a struggle or a fight. Just Missy's ComWatch.

Alex knew he couldn't let this happen anymore. There was no one left to count on. It was up to him to find the others and beat this thing, whatever it was.

"Commander Kellie! Paul! Missy! Rapper! Valerie!" Alex yelled into the hole, hoping to get some kind of answer. But none came.

"It's just you and me, Techno." Alex looked at the robot.

"I detect another human in there now," Techno noted, referring to Missy's added presence. "And the strawberry is still there. Do you think it's responsible for this?"

Alex scowled. "I doubt it, but we're going to run a complete checkup on you if—er, *when*—we get back."

Techno beeped. Alex looked down at Missy's ComWatch and turned it around in his hand. The protruding side buttons pressed against his fingers as the clear face mirrored back at him. He flipped it over and rubbed his fingers over the back side. A small indentation on the top of the back cover caught Alex's attention. He smiled briefly.

"I've got an idea." Alex popped off the back cover of Missy's ComWatch with his thumbnail, revealing a thin wire wrapped around the circumference of the ComWatch's inner workings. It was the wire used to charge up the watch. One end was attached to the ComWatch's small, rechargeable battery, the other end would attach to the charger. But Alex had other ideas for it.

With a *snap!*, Alex broke off the end of the wire attached to the watch. Then, he pulled the rubbery covering off the other end. Seconds later, Alex was stretching the bare-ended wire straight, working out any kinks.

After popping off the back of his own watch, too, he carefully twisted one end of the wire around the base of his watch's transmission chip. The other end he twisted around the metal base of the transmission chip in Missy's watch. Then, carefully placing both down, face-up on the floor, Alex turned both ComWatches on.

Ffft-zzzap! Alex's face appeared on both screens. "Huh?" he stammered. Then he realized why: Before Missy had entered the hole, they had programmed each ComWatch to pick up the other watch's view...and both watches were currently viewing Alex!

"Hey, good-looking," he said suavely. His video twins echoed back the compliment.

Alex switched both watches to link to Commander Kellie's watch. He was hoping that with the transmission chips linked, he would be able to transmit and receive over a longer distance. He was hoping to double the power of the ComWatches. He still wouldn't be able to communicate outside the walls, but if Commander Kellie and the others were in the room beyond, he figured he might at least be able to get a clue about their whereabouts.

The watches crackled. Alex rolled the fine-tuning switch with his fingertip. With each slowly passing groove, the crackling increased. According to a circular graph in the corner of the ComWatch face, his range of communication was increasing ever so slightly with each click...but the farther it went, the more "staticky" it became.

"-lex?"

Alex flinched. Was that—?

"*Pffft*-elp! P-*pffft*-*pffft*-*pffft*-app-*pffft*-*pffft*-ence-*pffft*."

Something was coming through! It sounded like Commander Kellie's voice! But something was wrong.

"Commander Kellie! Commander Kellie!" Alex cried into the ComWatches. "Can you hear me?"

The watches snapped, crackled and popped. A message proclaiming **"INTERFERENCE"** blinked on and off. He switched the ComWatches over to Paul's frequency. There was nothing but blackness and silence, but then—

"Alex! *Pffft*-*pffft*-ly need hel-*pffft*."

"Paul! Where are you? What's happening? Does the mysterious presence have you?"

Suddenly the screen flickered and Paul's face, dimly lit by his flashlight, eerily flashed on the watch faces. It blinked on and off as the signal went in and out.

"*Pffft*-ome in he-*pffft*." Paul's face vanished and Rapper's appeared in its place. "We n-*pffft*-elp!" In the background, Alex heard a cracking sound, like a sledgehammer ripping apart cement—and then he heard a scream from one of the girls. As suddenly as they had come on, the faces vanished from the screen. Alex tried for another 10 minutes to re-establish contact, but nothing worked. **"INTERFERENCE."**

"CONNECTION LOST."

But at least he knew they were still alive...

"Well," Alex said finally, admitting that he was ready to try something new, "I don't know what's responsible for this, but we have to rescue the others."

"Are you going in?" Techno inquired.

"I don't see any other way," Alex answered. "But I really need to try something different. If I just walk straight in like everyone else, I'm sure to have the same thing happen to me."

Think, Alex, think! he thought to himself. Second Corinthians 10:5 came to his mind—"Take captive every thought to make it obedient to Christ." He knew he had to rely on the peace of Christ to control his thinking and put himself above the situation. He felt a chill and realized he was still barefoot from complying with Missy's idea. He slid his socks back on. He grabbed his shoes, placed them back on his feet, too, and laced them up.

There wasn't much left available to use in helping the others. Alex had his Academy-issued flashlight, two ComWatches, half of Missy's clothes and a robot that was too big to fit into the hole. Down each side of the corridor was a locked door—way too thick to get the attention of anyone on the other side.

"Oh, I don't know," Alex whispered to himself answering the obvious question: *What do I do next?*

He sat down beside the hole with a feeling of defeat kicking to be acknowledged. Though he didn't feel much like it, Alex softly began to pray in the spirit. Techno didn't stir. Alex ran his fingers along the outside of the hole, feeling the jagged edges. To Alex's fingers, the rough hole felt like a portrait of his life. It was well-rounded, like Alex, but rough around the edges.

Alex didn't have a grand life story like the other Superkids. Paul was an orphan and a rebel dirt-biker before he asked God to become part of his life. Rapper had been a member of an inner-city gang before he made Jesus his Lord and left the streets for Superkid Academy. Missy came from a rich family and had thought she was so good she didn't need anything or anyone. Then she met Jesus and came to Superkid Academy—and discovered how empty her life really had been without the Lord. Valerie, on the other hand, grew up on a little island—Calypso Island—where her parents were missionaries. Her family saw more prejudice, rebellion and outright anger than most families ever see—but through it all, Valerie made the decision to follow Jesus no matter what the cost.

And then there was Alex.

His parents were Christians and he had followed Jesus for as long as he could remember. His family was successful and happy. He went to school, got good grades and enjoyed sports. The worst tragedy he'd ever faced was some other kids making fun of him because he was short—not exactly anything he could write a book about.

He was jagged around the edges sometimes—unsure of himself and a little shy. And now he was feeling entirely helpless. He picked at the edge of the hole with his thumbnail. A small pebble popped off and bounced on the ground. Little granules of dust fell from where the small rock had been.

Alex let out a long breath when the dust fell. He felt like a little grain of dust—floating, alone and insignificant. And nothing scared him more than realizing that on the other side of the black hole in the wall was some sort of mysterious presence that could make him disappear, too. If only he were bigger than it was...

Greater is He that is in you, than he that is in the world.

That's right, Alex thought as the Holy Spirit reminded him of 1 John 4:4—a verse his mom always read to him from her tattered *King James* Bible. *Jesus inside me is greater than any mysterious presence!*

If God is for you, no one can be against you.

"That's right—Romans 8:31," Alex quoted aloud. "Now if only God could show up personally!"

Psalm 22:3 says that God inhabits the praises of His people.

Alex thought about what the Holy Spirit was telling him. He had learned about Psalm 22:3 the past week in the Superkids' morning study time with Commander Kellie. The Bible says God inhabits the praises of His people.

That means when one of His children begins to praise, God comes on the scene! And when God comes on the scene...Alex knew right then—right there—what he needed to do.

Alex pulled himself up, knelt and lifted up his hands. After a moment of silence, he began to sing a song to the Lord. It was a song that came boldly out of his spirit—a song he had never heard before.

I'll remember You in all I do
I know You will give me success
All my trust I place in You
I'll depend on You through this test

For You are my God
Inhabit my praises
Rise up in me
Your voice I hear

You protect me, give us all safety
You are my resting place every day
Angels are in charge of me
Holy Spirit, show me the way

For You are my God
Inhabit my praises
Rise up in me
You've removed my fear

Alex prayed in the spirit, interceding for his friends, and then he grew quiet and listened to the Holy Spirit speak to his spirit. The Holy Spirit stirred Alex to remember all that had recently happened.

Only two hours ago, Alex remembered hiding behind the others as Paul detonated the explosive, causing the hole to be blasted in the wall. What was on the other side was a mystery, but everyone was eager to discover the answer.

He remembered the BANG! that hit his ears when Paul set it off. He remembered Commander Kellie's gratified expression for a job well done. He remembered Techno reporting that there was only oxygen and dust inside. He even recalled Valerie brushing some of the dust from her hair and Missy muttering something about the...

The dust.

There was a lot of dust...but Alex remembered that it didn't just come from the hole. Alex turned around and looked at the fixture beside the hole. *A vent.* Not a big one, but maybe big enough to crawl through...and if he could crawl through it, he could find help...

Thank You, Holy Spirit! Alex prayed. Then he stood up and walked over to his robotic friend.

"Techno!" he yelped. "I need your help."

Alex instructed Techno to grab hold of the ventilation grate with his metal claws and pull. The robot did as advised and with one good, hard yank, the grate cracked off the wall and revealed a dusty tunnel beyond.

Alex stuck his head in and could see another grate on the opposite side. *That's where the dust came through to get into the hallway,* he thought to himself. He slid back out.

"Techno, can you bring up your dome-map again?" he prompted. With a buzz, the blue-lined, holographic map of Superkid Academy filled Techno's domed head.

"OK. Now can you highlight the ventilation system?"

In a flash, red lines intersected the blue layout, revealing an intricate ventilation structure. "Excellent," Alex applauded.

"Thank you," Techno replied. "I'm also programmed with a complete analysis of 63 different ways to dissect frogs."

Alex winced. "I'll keep that in mind."

Alex traced his finger along the dome and found the hallway they were in next to the secret room he had found. A red line indicated the ventilation tunnel they were standing beside.

"This will be tough to memorize," Alex said, biting his lower lip.

"I'll lead you through," Techno offered.

"You can't fit in this air vent!" Alex argued, "It's barely big enough for *me!*"

Techno beeped and rolled over to the vent. "If I speak into here, it will echo." Alex could hear Techno's digital voice echoing in the vent as he finished the sentence.

"It's like when me and my brother used to talk to each other through the vents in our little house when we were growing up!" Alex cheered. "Good thinking, Techno!"

"I'm also programmed with complete scripts to every Wichita Slim movie ever created."

"I'll keep that in mind next time I'm in the mood for a Western," Alex said. Techno rolled away from the vent. Alex tried to communicate with his friends one last time, but nothing resulted. He shoved the ComWatches into his pants pocket. Then, with a big gulp of breath and an even bigger gulp of courage, Alex entered the ventilation shaft.

Alex was down on all fours, practically having to crawl on his stomach to move effectively. Now that he'd entered the boxy, metallic crawl space, he knew there was no turning back. He couldn't turn around if he wanted to. He had to keep himself from thinking about how closed in he was. He knew if he needed to, he could always crawl backward through the tunnel and back to the hallway, but that would probably be more difficult than going forward.

Alex crawled away from the vent at a sharp, upward angle until he came to a split in the path. He reasoned he was near the top of the wall. "Techno, I'm at a junction. Left or right?"

Techno bleeped and then his echoing voice signaled, "Go right. The other way is a dead end."

Alex slipped around the corner, to his discomfort, and kept moving along faithfully. For the first time it hit him how hungry he was.

Alex held his flashlight, set on medium beam, in front of himself with one hand and pulled himself through with the other. His sneakers scraped and pushed the sides of the tunnel with every inch. He had gone about 10 feet when he was faced with another decision.

"Techno, I'm at another junction!"

This place is a maze, he thought.

"Go right again," Techno ordered. His voice was slightly more faint than it had been. Alex wondered how much longer he'd be able to hear his technological friend. He turned right again and almost immediately came to a sharp slope.

"Techno, should I go up?" he shouted.

"Affirmative. The tunnel will put you right above the hidden room."

Great, Alex thought. *I wanted to be above the situation, but I didn't mean literally!* But Alex knew he needed to go this way. According to the map, the fastest route to freedom would be to travel over the hidden room and then crawl through another wall. It would put him next to one of Superkid Academy's main control rooms.

Alex shuffled along the path. It went up, up, up. Then it flattened out and twisted again and again. Many times, he found himself curling his whole body around the curves. He couldn't recollect being briefed on this kind of work for his Academy entrance exam.

At the end of one of the tightest curves, the tunnel sloped down sharply. Alex held his breath and pulled himself down headfirst, working to keep himself from sliding down too fast. If it had been any steeper, he would have been free falling.

Alex continued to crawl forward until suddenly the smooth surface of the path changed. In front of him, Alex found a small hook attached to a long, rusty metal grate. He froze. He would have to crawl over the grate to get to the other side—and he wasn't sure if it would support him. "Techno, there's a 5-foot grate in front of me and then a junction on the other side of it. What should I do?"

He heard the gurgling of the robot's voice, but couldn't make out what he was saying. He had gone too far to hear Techno clearly. He thought about going back, but decided against it since it meant crawling backward, up the remarkably steep slope he'd just come down. He would just have to go over the grate.

Crossing over the grate meant that Alex would be crawling directly over the hidden room. Alex peered through the brownish-orange, metal bars to see if he could see anything below. It was pitch black…though he could see the dim pinpoint of the hole they had blasted through earlier. Best as he could judge, he was over the center of the room.

At one point, he even thought he heard hushed voices, but when he called out the names of his friends through the latticework, no one answered. He put down his flashlight for a moment. Awkwardly, Alex pulled his arm back and maneuvered his hand down into his pocket. He grabbed the duo-ComWatch device he had created and pulled it up in front of him. He had to keep trying.

Alex switched the watches to Commander Kellie's frequency. Nothing. He tried Paul's frequency. Still nothing. Next, he tried Valerie's frequency.

"—back!" *Yes!* It was Valerie. She was shining her flashlight in her face so Alex could see her. He flipped around his flashlight so she could see him.

"Valerie!" Alex shouted into the watches. From her limited lighting, her face looked olive green in the ComWatch screen.

"Alex—you're very clear! Where *pffft* you?"

"I'm above you, I think....Where are you? Are you safe from the presence—" Valerie's face disappeared and Commander Kellie's took its place.

"Alex, good work. But we ne-*pffft* your help—and fast."

Alex was wide-eyed. "Why? What is it? What can I do?"

CRRRAAAACCCCCKKKK!!!!!!

A booming, ripping sound burst from the ComWatches and filled the chamber. Alex's arms jolted in surprise. His hands yanked apart in reflex and let go of the watches. They flew forward together and danced over the grate. One stayed on top, but the other dropped through and hung in midair—dangling only by the thin wire attached between the watches. Alex froze for a moment and gulped.

Reaching forward, careful not to knock the grate, Alex grabbed hold of the watch on top and lifted it. Gingerly, he raised the second watch up. With his other hand, Alex took hold of the wire between the two and let out a long breath. Now all he had to do was get the second watch through the grate. Carefully, he pulled up again. The watch band, spread out on both sides of the base, tapped against the grate. The wire Alex had so meticulously twisted around the transmitter base popped off and the watch disappeared. Down into the room. Alex listened but never heard it hit the floor. He looked at his ComWatch and it simply displayed the message **"UNABLE TO CONNECT."** *Great.* He wrapped it around his wrist.

Alex knew he had to go on. Got to help. Got to find a way to help his friends. They were in serious trouble. They were counting on him. There was no time to waste.

Before making an attempt to cross, Alex checked the hook on the grate. It was firmly linked through a metal loop, but could be easily removed. Using his flashlight, he saw hinges on the other side. He reasoned that if he unhooked the latch, it would swing open into the room. But Alex was careful to leave it shut—he needed it closed so he could use it as a bridge to the other side.

Carefully, like a spider working its way across a web, Alex started forward. He inched himself around the latch and pulled himself over the grate until finally his hands reached the hinges. *Only a little way to go,* he thought. But then he stopped midway. Directly in front of him was another juncture. He had to go left or right. *Which way? Which way?* he wondered.

Suddenly the grate creaked.

Alex looked through the bars to the expanse below. He didn't want to fall through, whatever he did. Best he could estimate, the floor would be about 30 feet down.

It would be a long fall, and not one he wanted to take. He could just imagine plunging right onto a giant strawberry...or worse yet, dropping right on top of the mysterious presence that had enveloped the others.

"Father God, please guide me," he prayed.

Take the right tunnel, the Lord replied to his spirit.

Without questioning, Alex groped for the right tunnel. He pulled himself slowly...steadily...

Creak!

Alex got his arms up into the right tunnel, but suddenly felt something pulling at his shoe. He looked down and gasped as he realized his shoelace was caught on the hook that kept the grate shut. With every lunge forward, he was jiggling the hook out of the latch. Carefully, slowly, Alex pulled his arms out of the passageway and with a little maneuvering managed to get one down near his shoe. The grate creaked again. He wasn't sure how long it would hold him.

Alex's fingers could barely reach the wayward lace. He had to suck in his stomach and bend his upper body down to attempt getting his hand closer to his foot. Finally, his first two fingers grabbed hold of the lace and slid it gently out around the hook. Alex sighed. At least the grate wouldn't be opening.

Creeeeeak!

But that didn't mean it wouldn't fall through! Without another moment's hesitation, Alex pulled his arms back in front of him and pushed himself forward so hard that he nearly leapt.

Wham! He landed on smooth ground again. He looked at the grate behind him. It stayed in place. His heart pounded from excitement. He took a deep sigh of relief. Then he gulped.

He was in the wrong tunnel.

"I wanted to take the *right* tunnel!" Alex shouted aloud. He couldn't believe it. He was so concerned with getting over the grate that he went the wrong way. Or *was* it the wrong way? He was sure he'd heard from the Lord, but maybe both ways would lead to the same place. After all, it would be a lot of trouble to turn around...and that grate probably wouldn't support him a second time. So, with a little reluctance, Alex went ahead and forged his way through the left tunnel.

But he couldn't help but feel that he was heading in the wrong direction.

All Alex could think about was getting to the end. He was feeling cramped and crowded—like standing with too many people in an elevator. He found himself groaning about the situation at one point, but caught himself. He decided instead to sing praise to God as he crawled.

Holy, holy, holy
Lord, above all You are holy
Worthy, worthy, worthy
Father, You are worthy to be praised

It felt good to praise. It helped Alex keep his mind off the close walls. And he could feel courage grow in his heart.

I want to be holy like You, Lord
Make me more like You
I want to be holy like You, Lord
You are worthy, I worship You

Up ahead, Alex saw a sharp curve. Wiggling and pushing, he moved around it. And then he stopped. There was nowhere to go. It was a dead end.

▲ ▲ ▲

As much as he didn't want to do it, Alex had to go back and take the right-hand tunnel. He thought about trying to turn around, but the walls were too cramped. He would have to crawl backward through the passageway.

Shining his flashlight beam back over his shoulder, Alex pushed himself back around the bend. He could hardly believe he'd come all this way to find a dead end. *I should have followed the Lord's leading,* he thought.

Going back the way he came was much harder than he thought it would be. Between balancing the flashlight, looking over his shoulder and groping with his feet, he was surprised he made it back as fast as he did.

Soon, he saw the familiar, rusty grate looming behind him. He put down his flashlight, closed his eyes and wiped his forehead on his sleeve. He felt exhausted—and he wasn't sure how much farther he still had to go.

He scolded himself once more for finding the room in the first place and setting the whole adventure in motion. Reluctantly, he grabbed his flashlight again and scooted closer and closer to the grate.

Just as he thought, there was no way to get around to the other tunnel without putting at least half of his body over the grate. So slowly, he trudged on.

His feet hit the grate first. *Creak!* Alex winced—*not this again!* He made a promise to himself that he would do his best to keep his full body weight from resting on the rusted grate.

Before moving any farther, Alex turned from his stomach onto his side so that his back faced the wall creating the junction. Then, slowly and carefully, he inched around the wall.

Alex let out a breath of victory when his legs, from the knees down, curled around the bend. He was one-fourth of the way there. Then a realization hit him—if he curled around like this, he would be in the right passageway—but he would be backward! The only way to get in facing frontward was to put his legs straight down, put himself over the grate again and then crawl forward. Alex huffed.

Feeling the aching in his legs, he stretched them out over the grate. To Alex's relief, nothing happened. Then, once again, he pushed himself down over the grate. It creaked a little, but didn't seem to be losing support. Alex felt his hip slide over a hinge and he rolled over onto his stomach again. He inched back more.

His stomach slid down onto the grate, followed by his torso and finally his shoulders. He had made it! Now, to get into the right tunnel...

Alex put his head in the right-hand tunnel and smiled. He was almost there....Slowly he pulled himself up.

CREAK! He froze all movement. Nothing happened.

Alex began to crawl again.

CREAK! He stopped again. He would have to take another leap into the tunnel, like he did the last time. But at least he would be heading the right way.

Alex counted *one...two...three!* and pushed himself up.

Click! His shoe hit the metal latch—Alex watched over his shoulder as the hook popped out. Suddenly, beneath him, the grate swung open. Alex felt himself pulled down by the force of gravity. He dropped his flashlight in the right-hand tunnel. And with nothing beneath him but the enveloping darkness, he fell.

In a swift movement, Alex grabbed on to the end of the grate just before he plunged past it. His fingers burned as he held on to the edge of the cold, metal grid. He could feel himself swinging freely in the air as he struggled to hang on. He barely saved himself from a nasty fall. Above him, he could see his flashlight shining, casting eerie shadows.

With all the strength he could muster, Alex pulled himself up a few rungs. His hands were covered with brownish-orange corrosion, making them rough and slippery at the same time.

CREAK! He wasn't sure how long this grate would support him, but he had to do something fast. Pulling his left foot up, Alex placed it on the metal ring at the bottom of the swinging grate that had held the hook moments earlier. Alex gained enough support to pull himself up farther. Inch by inch, Alex lifted himself. He was finally high enough to grab hold of the flashlight above with one hand. Again he thought he heard the gurgling of voices beneath him.

Bible verses about having courage and not fearing rose up in his spirit. "God did not give me a spirit of fear. He gave me a spirit of power and of love and of a sound mind," he said, quoting 2 Timothy 1:7. He looked up to see how much farther he had to go before reaching far enough to pull himself back in the tunnel. It was only about a foot, but it looked like a mile. He could only imagine what was beneath him. He shined his flashlight down and gasped at the sight. Below him, the room was filled with brilliant, vibrant color.

Squinting in disbelief, Alex looked down to see huge bubbles of red, blue, green and yellow. His mind trailed back to what Valerie had said just before she disappeared...something about "how beautiful" it was... Alex pulled his eyes away from it. He knew that he was over the area where the mysterious presence resided—

or whatever it was that captured Commander Kellie and the other Superkids.

"I will *not* be afraid," he said, more as a form of prayer than a reality. With true grit, he pulled himself upward. His fingers still burned, his knuckles were in pain and his body ached. He watched as his dark hand slowly began to slip. Then he heard a *snap!* and he knew the little metal ring he was standing on had broken. He was free-falling.

Alex's flashlight went flying and his feet buckled underneath him as he came crashing down. He hit what felt like pockets of air, then he plunged into something big and fluffy, then he dropped onto the hard floor. *POW! POW! POW! CRASH! SMASH! BOOM!* Sounds enveloped him. He came down hard on his left leg, crunching it under the weight of his body. But Alex's mind wasn't on his hurting leg...all he could think about was the presence that probably lurked nearby. He looked all around, but couldn't see anything. It was pitch black.

His hands and face were covered with something sticky and his arm was wet. With the exception of his left leg, his body felt slightly bruised, but fine—something had broken his fall. Alex reached out around him, but retracted his arm when his hand hit a clump of goopy, sticky slime. It was the same goo that was all over him. Whatever it was, Alex didn't want to stick around to find out. In an attempt to raise himself up, Alex's hurting, left knee slipped out from under him. *SMACK!* It hit something. Pain shot through Alex's leg.

"Owwww!" he cried, wincing at the pain. His leg was throbbing and numb at the same time. He could barely move it. Between the fall and the sudden collision with his knee, he wasn't sure if he could go anywhere.

Carefully, he reached out his fingertips to the object his knee smashed into. It was a long cylinder.

My flashlight!

Alex grabbed it immediately. It was time to find out where he was and what had happened. It was time to shine the light on everything. He tapped the "on" button and couldn't believe what he saw.

Nothing. He *saw nothing.* The flashlight was broken. Thoughts raced through Alex's mind. *What do I do now? I can't see my own hand in front of my face! How will I find the others? I can't move my leg! How will I find the way out? Will the mysterious presence find me before I get out? I don't think I'll ever eat another strawberry in my lifetime. If only I could see* something!

Alex tried to pull himself up on his good leg, but it hurt too much to stand. He dropped back down on all fours and prayed his good knee would stop shaking. Then he saw his first glimmer of hope. About 200 feet away, there was a small, crude circle of light shining into the room. It didn't take long for Alex to realize it was the hole they'd blasted through only two and a half hours ago. It seemed like days had passed since then. Now, if only he could do it over again. If only he had never found this secret, old NME room hidden within the Academy. If only...

Worn and slightly bruised, Alex began to crawl toward the hole, dragging his weak leg—but then he froze. His own thoughts stopped him in his tracks. Like a blow to the face, Alex realized that going to the hole wouldn't do him any good. Then what? The doors outside were locked. The only way out was over the room... and he couldn't go that way again because the grate — his bridge — had fallen through and broken.

The only thing Alex could do was hope to solve this mystery. Maybe if he discovered what had happened to the others, he could figure out an answer. Maybe he could find someone else's flashlight...

Alex bowed his head. And in the middle of the blackest darkness he'd ever been in, Alex forced himself to stop shaking and he praised God, singing a song the Holy Spirit put in his heart.

Lord, You give me victory
Lord, You give me eyes so I can see
Lord, You set me wholly free
When, Lord, You gave Your life for me

And now You're here
Yes, Your presence is here with me
Guiding me, helping me, showing me...

Alex stopped singing and chuckled.

That's it, isn't it? he asked God. **You** *are with me. I don't have to be afraid. So what if there* **is** *a mysterious presence...***Your presence** *is with me. And You are* **God!** *I've been acting like* **You** *are the One who is mysterious — like* **You** *are the One I'm just hoping will help me. But You* **will** *help me! Psalm 46:1 says that* **You** *are my* *protection and strength. You **always** help in times of trouble. There's no mystery to that! You said it in Your Word and it's true. So in the Name of Jesus, I'm going to count on You and Your anointing **now**. Father, show me the way. I'm putting my trust—I'm putting my **faith** —in You.*

Like a surge of electrical power, Alex felt the strength of the Lord fill him. He used the sudden energy to praise the Lord more—this time in the spirit, by singing words the Holy Spirit gave him—words Alex didn't even recognize. He was no longer afraid. He was going to find the answer—because God's presence was with him.

Suddenly his weak leg began to tingle, then it burned like fire was running through his bones. Amazingly, it didn't hurt in the least. In fact, it felt...healing. The sensation subsided and Alex bent his leg—not even a tinge of pain reared up. Alex jumped to his feet. His left leg supported him just as well—no, *better* than it had before. *Healed!*

He got ecstatic as it registered how the power of praise had brought him joy...and the joy was strength— even to his body. *Yes! Praise You, Jesus! Nehemiah 8:10 says, "The joy of the Lord is my strength!"* Then Alex remembered something else. Something else that happens when a person praises the Lord. *Psalm 9:3— "My enemies turn back."* Satan has to run!

"God's Spirit, who is in me, is greater than the devil, who is in the world!" Alex shouted, citing 1 John 4:4.

"Satan, I command your forces to step aside. I loose the angels of God to help me find my friends!"

Suddenly, like the bursting of a comet, Alex's flashlight came on and shined into his face. Alex jumped and then smiled confidently. He quickly examined himself and saw that he was indeed covered with goo. From head to toe, there was pinkish-purple goop smothered all over his body. It smelled sweet like...strawberries? Alex wondered if he had landed on top of the gigantic strawberry, bursting it under his weight. He hoped not—that would be too gross.

Alex took a sideways step and lifted the flashlight to examine the room around him—then he abruptly froze. Something had hold of his foot.

"Don't move an inch," it whispered.

Under most circumstances, Alex would have been scared to have a giant strawberry attacking his Achilles' tendon, but with the power of the Lord surging through him, it didn't even faze him.

"You'd better let go!" Alex was confident. "Not only is the Lord on my side, but I'm known for my mean appetite for strawberries."

"How can you think of food at a time like this?" the voice said in a hushed shout. This time it sounded familiar.

"Missy?" Alex asked. He shined his flashlight at his foot. It was captured by a hand...a hand sticking out of the floor. "Huh?" He brushed his flashlight beam around the hand. There it was—inches away from the hand was a head...Missy's head! Sticking out of the floor! Odd as it looked, Alex wasn't scared. He confidently bent down to examine it closer. "Alex, thank God you're here!" it shouted. Suddenly, the hand around his ankle became very heavy and another hand popped up out of the solid ground. Something grabbed the back of Alex's head and pulled down hard. Alex braced himself for the sudden impact of his forehead with the floor. It never came. Instead, his head kept going down—past the surface of the floor.

When Alex opened his eyes, he suddenly saw four flashlight beams shooting straight at him. Handclaps and cheers followed.

"What'd you expect? A man-eating strawberry?" Rapper shouted up at Alex. They were in a deep room with walls angled outward and a cement floor that was considerably cracked. He looked around and realized all his friends were accounted for. Missy was standing on Paul's shoulders, her head sticking out of the ceiling.

"You're under the floor," Alex stated, with a hint of a smile. Now that he saw his friends, alive and well, his hope increased even more.

"No kidding," Rapper replied, dryly.

Commander Kellie affirmed, "We're *all* under the floor—in this old, NME trap. And we need you to get us—" *CRRRR*...The concrete floor of the trap shook under their weight. "We need you to get us out fast, Alex. This old floor's been ripping away ever since I first got trapped in here."

Alex processed it for a minute. "But how did you—"

"We fell through that holographic false floor," Paul said flatly, pointing at the ceiling. "The one your head is stuck through now. But don't worry—no one's hurt."

"We just couldn't get out without any support from above," Valerie added. "And that holographic door somehow blocked us from hearing each other."

"So you—"

CRRRR...

Missy pulled her head back down and interrupted Alex's next thought. *"We'll explain everything as soon as you help us out!"*

"OK" Alex agreed, understanding. "How far up can you guys get?"

"Well, we were able to get Missy up high enough to reach the edge of the floor, but that's it," Commander Kellie rationalized. "With you pulling from above, we should all be able to get out, one by one."

"But we can't put more than two people on top of one another," Rapper added. "It's too much weight in one spot. The floor can't handle it."

"You tried it?" Alex wondered. Rapper moved his flashlight beam over to another side of the floor. The cement had completely crumbled away and all Alex could see was darkness beyond. Apparently they *had* tried it...and failed. That must have been the loud crack he heard earlier.

CRRRR...

And if he didn't hurry and help, he was likely to hear more!

"We need to make this fast!" Paul shouted. Alex raised up through the holographic floor, pushing up with his hands. Missy looked up at Alex, through the imaginary surface. On instinct, Alex set his flashlight aside. The room was darker again, with only his flashlight shining, but Alex knew there was nothing to fear. He reached down, solidly grabbed on to Missy's hands and braced himself. He shook his head. Lifting the full weight of another person wasn't his specialty.

"You can do it—" Missy began to say.

CRRRR...Alex could hear the floor of the trap trembling.

"Let's go!" Paul shouted. "Or this will be a short victory!"

Inwardly, Alex thanked God for the strenuous workouts he had at the Academy. But still, he wasn't sure if he was prepared to lift her all the way up. It was a miracle that he found them in the first place. It would take another miracle for him to get them out.

For a moment, he thought she might slip—his hands were still covered with the pinkish-purple goo from his earlier fall. But her grip became stronger. She apparently wasn't going to give up. Alex pulled hard.

"Praise...You...Jesus!" Alex forced out with tight breaths.

Suddenly, like a whip, Missy shot up toward Alex. With her knee, she got over the rim of the trap. Then with a kick, Missy arched her foot up against the other side of the trap and threw herself out of the hole. She tumbled onto the floor, catching Alex in her wake. She laughed and shrieked, excited to be free. Without another second passing, she threw her arms around Alex and gave him a big, bear hug.

"My hero!" she shouted. Alex's heart welled up within him and he could feel the warmth of his face blushing. Then Missy backed away and looked at her clothes, now covered in the goo that was all over Alex.

"This is definitely a look I haven't tried before," she admitted, flashing her toothy smile.

Alex couldn't contain his laughter. "I think I popped the giant strawberry."

Missy laughed, too. "That's really gross."

Alex shrugged his shoulders dramatically.

CRRRR...

"Let me help you get the others out," Missy offered. Alex nodded.

Valerie popped her head through the holographic trap next and Alex and Missy each grabbed one of her hands. Still sticky with slime, Alex anchored his weight, and with Missy's help, he pulled Valerie up and out easily.

Paul insisted that Commander Kellie and Rapper get out before him, and as each one came, they joined the effort from above, making the next lift easier. But the floor of the trap didn't stop cracking. It was slowly ripping away from the stress.

Finally, with Paul alone down below, they had to lower someone down for him to grab onto so he could be lifted up.

"Let me go," Alex offered. With the strength of the Lord rushing through him like a mighty river, he was ready for more.

Commander Kellie nodded and a moment later she and Missy, Rapper and Valerie grabbed his legs and lowered him down, headfirst. Alex felt a sizzle of adrenaline zip through his body from his head to his feet as he was lowered through the false floor.

Paul looked up and then looked at the floor again with his light. Alex watched as he saw it cracking before his eyes.

"Hurry, guys, hurry!" Paul shouted. Alex reached down as far as he could, hoping and praying the others had a good hold on his legs. Paul reached up...closer...closer.

CRRRR...

The floor continued to crack. Not in just one place now, but across the whole floor, like an army of creeping snakes.

Alex reached. Paul reached. But they couldn't quite get...

CRRRRRRRAAAAAACCCCCKKKKK! Alex closed his eyes as the deafening noise blew through the small trap and the floor fell away. Sticky air blew up and smacked Alex in the face.

"PAUL!" Alex opened his eyes. And looking straight up at him was his friend...hanging on tightly to Alex's hand in midair.

"Up! Up! Pull us up!" Paul shouted.

Commander Kellie and the Superkids pulled with all their might, dragging Alex and Paul from the trap. Alex felt the warmth of victory as they were lifted up from the trap, up through the floor, up to freedom. In moments, at last, everyone was on solid ground.

"That did wonders for my nails," Missy muttered with a smile.

Commander Kellie gave Alex a hug. "You are *definitely* a hero," she said, embracing Alex and patting his back. Alex felt like he could take on a mountain. Then she backed away and said, "I guess it's time for you to know what this was all supposed to be about."

"Supposed to be about?" Alex asked.

Everyone turned off their flashlights, except Rapper. He tapped his flashlight on high power, ran to the far side of the room—opposite from where they'd blasted the hole—and stopped. Then he turned off his flashlight and everything went dark. Then, right after Alex heard a beep, everything lit up.

"Surprise!" Paul, Missy, Rapper, Valerie and Commander Kellie shouted less-than-enthusiastically. As Alex's eyes focused, he saw the room was old, but aglow with bright streamers, balloons and a huge banner draped across the middle that proclaimed, "HAPPY BIRTHDAY ALEX! WE LOVE YOU!"

Alex pulled at the goo on his shirt and realized it was not only pink and purple, but it was also thick and... sugary. Strawberry frosting...mixed with little bits of strawberry cake. Alex had fallen directly on top of it when he'd plummeted from the ceiling.

"Not much left of your cake," Valerie said, giggling. Rapper reached down and picked up a tattered piece of red rubber.

"Not much left of your balloons, either," he added. It hit Alex that the balloons were the colorful bubbles which had broken his fall on the way down.

"You're soaked," Alex said, looking at Rapper.

"Yeah, I bumped into the punch bowl because I was too busy looking at the streamers."

"Stream...ers." Alex realized he had misunderstood the message about the stream earlier.

He giggled at himself, still a little bit on edge. "You guys did all this for *me?*" Alex wiped a clump of strawberry frosting from his ear. Paul ran back to the middle of the room.

"Yep, we did it for you," he said, and then bent down and pushed his hand through the holographic trap. His hand looked like it was disappearing into the solid ground. "But we sure hadn't counted on *this* being here."

Commander Kellie laughed. "You never know what you're going to find in an old NME building."

"The plan," Rapper explained, "was for us all to come in here, one by one, and then yell, 'Surprise!' when you entered. We wanted to give you a birthday you'd never forget."

"Well, it's been *that*," Alex offered.

"But then when we lost communication with Commander Kellie, we thought something might have gone wrong," Rapper said.

"Yeah, but we didn't know for sure," Valerie threw in. "It wasn't until Rapper and I got caught in the trap ourselves that we realized something was wrong for sure...and by then it was too late."

Missy giggled. "So I came in hoping to turn on the lights, but I couldn't reach the switch—clear on the other side of the room—while holding on to our short clothesline. So I let go. And then *I* hit the trap. It was right in our path between the hole we blasted and the 'party zone!'"

Alex shook his head. He couldn't believe all his friends had gone through for him. And to think that he almost gave up his search...but he didn't. He wasn't going to let some mysterious—

"Hey, wait!" Alex shouted, suddenly remembering. "What about the *mysterious presence?* Commander Kellie said she saw something mysterious. Some kind of presence. What about that?"

The commander smiled and pointed her index finger at a big crate. The Superkids all smiled. Cautiously, Alex approached the crate. He circled it once, and then, cautiously grabbing hold of the splintering wood, he lifted up the lid. His eyes grew as big as meatballs when he looked inside. One atop another they lay. Six diversely shaped boxes. Each one covered in metallic paper that shined in the light. "You mean...*this* is the mysterious—"

"Presents," Commander Kellie said, finishing Alex's thought. It was hard for Alex to believe. All this time, he thought there was some creature—some gigantic strawberry—lurking in the shadows. But he had just misunderstood the message.

"It's a good thing..." Alex muttered, his voice trailing off.

"You mean that it's a good thing there's no mysterious presence in here?" Paul wondered.

"No," Alex responded. "It's a good thing I learned about the power of praise. When I began to praise, God, who is stronger than any presence that could ever come against me, came on the scene. If I hadn't had that confidence, I might never have made it through and found you guys. But the Lord gave me the courage."

"And the victory," Commander Kellie said. "That's the power of praise."

"You are some super kid, Superkid," Paul said, roughing up Alex's hair.

"I'm glad you were available to be used by Him, Alex." Valerie winked. "If you hadn't been, we might not have made it...and our last memory might have been the smell of Missy's bare feet!"

Missy shot Valerie a wide smile. She threw her arms out and modeled her strawberry cake-covered clothes while wiggling her toes. "Hey, it's my new look!"

Alex burst out laughing and the whole group of friends joined in, relieved that their unexpected adventure was over.

"Orange you glad I didn't say banana again?" Missy said, jabbing Alex in the side.

"What?!" Alex scooped some vanilla ice cream from a container.

"That's the answer to the knock-knock joke. You asked, 'Who's there?' right before I fell in the trap. That's who. Get it?"

Alex shook his head. "Girl, you've got to come up with some new knock-knock jokes."

Alex's attention drew to the other side of the room when he heard a clunk and saw a door slide open.

"So there was another door to this room the whole time?" Alex asked.

"Yep," Paul said, nodding at the door as Techno wheeled through. "It leads to the janitor's closet in section 15. We accidentally found the door last week and thought this room would be perfect for your party. So, we didn't say anything and we set it up so you'd find it for yourself."

"The perfect surprise party," Valerie stated, "if it weren't for the trap left here by NME. We totally missed it when we were setting up for the party. Of course, at that time, there wasn't a hole blasted in the wall—and no reason to go in that direction."

Alex giggled as he busied himself with his ice cream.

"Missy Ashton?" a voice shouted. Missy put down her own scoop of vanilla ice cream and waved at a courier who had entered the room behind Techno. He rushed over to her and handed her a stack of envelopes and magazines. "Here's the mail you just called for."

"Yea!" she shouted. The courier left the room almost as fast as he had entered.

"Junk, junk, junk," Missy pronounced over each letter as she thumbed through it. "Junk, junk, ooh—a new beauty catalog." She put the catalog aside. "Junk, junk and ooh again! A letter from Mommy and Daddy." Missy always called her parents "Mommy and Daddy."

She carefully sliced open the back of the envelope with her thumbnail. She pulled out a check and waved it in the air. "Check for Missy!" she proclaimed. She stuffed it in her pants pocket and retrieved the letter from the envelope. It was written on fancy, floral stationery. She stuck the envelope behind the letter as she read silently.

Valerie was the first to notice Paul's face turning pale.

"Paul, what is it?!"

Paul jumped up, spilling his bowl of ice cream on the floor. He snatched the envelope from Missy, almost tearing the letter in the process. "Hey!" she cried.

"Paul?" Commander Kellie looked on with concern.

Paul held the envelope up in the light and peered closely at it. Stamped on the envelope by the post office, a red postmark that read "★★★ NAUTICAL ★★★ SEPTEMBER 9" glimmered in the light.

"Paul, are you OK?" Alex wondered.

Valerie approached Paul and shook his shoulder. "Paul?"

"You guys," he whispered at last. "You won't believe this."

The Superkids all waited for an answer.

"Are you going to tell us?" Alex wondered with a smile.

"Oh, sorry." Suddenly, Paul ran out of the room with the envelope.

Rapper laughed.

"Did I just miss something, or did he just steal my envelope?" Missy asked, twisting a lock of her hair. A moment later, Paul returned with not only the envelope, but also a worn blue, white and gold blanket.

"Paul, where'd you go?" Rapper put down his plastic bowl and utensil. "What's up?"

Paul spread the old blanket out on a clean section of the floor. He unrolled the corners and held it straight. The blanket was about 4 feet long and 4 feet wide. Bands of blue and white striped the cloth from the top to the bottom. Embroidered in the middle, in faded gold, was an emblem that made Alex gulp. There were three stars followed by the word "Nautical" and three more stars.

"The blanket's old," Paul whispered. "But do you see it?" He pointed to the gold lettering. "It's the same emblem that's on this envelope's postmark."

"So?" Missy wasn't impressed. "You've got a blanket from my hometown."

"No—I've got a blanket from *my* hometown."

"But you said the orphanage you grew up in was in some place called Sawyer..."

"It is!" Paul exclaimed. "But when I arrived at the orphanage as a baby, this blanket was delivered with me. I always thought 'Nautical' was just a brand name. I didn't realize it was a city. This is a *clue*, Missy! My parents must be from Nautical!"

"So..."

"So next week is our vacation week, right?"

Valerie piped up. "Yeah, we were all going to go visit my family on Calypso Island."

"Change in plans," Paul said, smiling. "You guys have fun...but I'm going to find the half of my life that's been missing...I'm going to find my parents!"

To be continued...

When Paul discovers a clue to his **past,**
his **future** will never be the same!

Look for *Commander Kellie and the Superkids*_{TM}
novel #2—

The Quest for the Second Half

by Christopher P.N. Maselli

Prayer for Salvation

Father God, I believe that Jesus is Your Son and that You raised Him from the dead for me. Jesus, I give my life to You. Right now, I make You the Lord of my life and choose to follow You forever. I love You and I know You love me. Thank You, Jesus, for giving me a new life. Thank You for coming into my heart and being my Savior. I am a child of God! Amen.

About the Author

For more than 15 years, Christopher Maselli has been sharing God's Word with kids through fiction. With a Master of Fine Arts in Writing, he is the author of more than 50 books, including the *Super Sleuth Investigators* mysteries, the *Amazing Laptop* series and the *Superkids Adventures*.

Chris lives in Fort Worth, Texas, with his wife and three children. His hobbies include running, collecting *"It's a Wonderful Life"* movie memorabilia and "way too much" computing.

Visit his website at ChristopherPNMaselli.com.

Other Products Available

Products Designed for Today's Children and Youth

And Jesus Healed Them All (confession book and CD gift package)
Baby Praise Board Book
Baby Praise Christmas Board Book
Load Up—A Youth Devotional
Over the Edge—A Youth Devotional
The Best of *Shout!* Adventure Comics
The *Shout!* Joke Book
Wichita Slim's Campfire Stories

Superkid Academy Children's Church Curriculum (DVD/CD curriculum)

* • Volume 1—My Father Loves Me!
* • Volume 2—The Fruit of the Spirit in You
* • Volume 3—The Sweet Life
* • Volume 4—Living in THE BLESSING
   • Volume 5—The Superkid Creed
   • Volume 6—The Superkid Creed II

Commander Kellie and the Superkids™ Books:

The *SWORD* Adventure Book
Commander Kellie and the Superkids™
   Solve-It-Yourself Mysteries
Commander Kellie and the Superkids™ Adventure Series:
   Middle Grade Novels by Christopher P.N. Maselli:

#1 The Mysterious Presence
#2 The Quest for the Second Half
#3 Escape From Jungle Island
#4 In Pursuit of the Enemy
#5 Caged Rivalry
#6 Mystery of the Missing Junk
#7 Out of Breath
#8 The Year Mashela Stole Christmas
#9 False Identity
#10 The Runaway Mission
#11 The Knight-Time Rescue of Commander Kellie

*Available in Spanish

We're Here for You!®

Your growth in God's WORD and victory in Jesus are at the very center of our hearts. In every way God has equipped us, we will help you deal with the issues facing you, so you can be the **victorious overcomer** He has planned for you to be.

The mission of Kenneth Copeland Ministries is about all of us growing and going together. Our prayer is that you will take full advantage of all The LORD has given us to share with you.

Wherever you are in the world, you can watch the *Believer's Voice of Victory* broadcast on television (check your local listings), the Internet at kcm.org or on our digital Roku channel.

Our website, **kcm.org,** gives you access to every resource we've developed for your victory. And, you can find contact information for our international offices in Africa, Asia, Australia, Canada, Europe, Ukraine and our headquarters in the United States.

Each office is staffed with devoted men and women, ready to serve and pray with you. You can contact the worldwide office nearest you for assistance, and you can call us for prayer at our U.S. number, +1-817-852-6000, 24 hours every day!

We encourage you to connect with us often and let us be part of your everyday walk of faith!

Jesus Is LORD!

Kenneth & Gloria Copeland

Kenneth and Gloria Copeland

CPSIA information can be obtained
at www.ICGtesting.com
Printed in the USA
FSOW04n2032230415
6646FS